SOUL SWAP OMNIBUS

SADIE THATCHER

CONTENTS

1

GODDESS WITHIN

"This is it," Claire said with awe as she looked upon the ancient sculpture. All of her hard work had finally paid off and she had finally found the lost Icon of the Eqo people.

Dr. Claire Donavan was an archeologist who had made it her life's work to study the Eqo civilization. The people had long ago disappeared, but the art and writings they had left behind were unlike anything seen elsewhere from the ancient world. It was truly phenomenal what the people thousands of years ago were able to accomplish. They put every other contemporary civilization to shame in their technological abilities.

The downfall of the Eqo civilization remained a mystery. One moment they were flourishing and the next they were gone, their cities emptied, their possessions left behind. The idea that they were actually aliens and their cities temporary outposts until the native human civilizations reached a high enough level to notice the aliens, causing them to leave, was a strong one, even in the actual scientific field and not just within the crackpot amateur archeologist community.

Claire did not know how it all happened, but she was not a

believer in the alien theory. The art, which included depictions of the Eqo people did not appear alien. Yes, the women pictured did appear to have overly large breasts, but that could have just been what the Eqo people valued. There were plenty of modern cultures that seemed to prefer women with larger breasts. Humans had not changed all that much over the years. Women all over were looked at for their beauty and that sometimes included really large breasts.

But the downfall of the Eqo civilization was not important to Claire at the moment. For her, she was much more interested in the religious structure of society. While her colleagues were concerned about the final days, Claire wanted to know more about how the people lived, how they worshiped. And that was what brought her to this point, working alone in a cave that was considered one of the earliest Eqo settlements, before they built their grand cities that time had buried.

Claire stepped forward and reached out toward the small statue. The lost Icon was lost because it had been removed from the main temple. Many assumed that treasure hunters had stolen it years ago. Others believed it had simply not stood up to the tests of time. But Claire believed it existed and now she had found it. From what she could tell, the Icon had been returned to its birthplace.

The stone of the round statue was made of the same material as the cave itself. The pillar it stood on looked like it had been carved from an even larger rock that had been there all along.

Not that the finding of the cave and this particular cavern had been easy. A collapsed area of the cave had blocked off the cavern. It was unclear if it was from geological shifting or if the cave had been collapsed on purpose in an effort to protect the contents of the cavern. After weeks of digging, alone, Claire had finally found what she was looking for.

However, Claire did not make immediate contact with the Icon. She held her hand back, afraid to touch it. The Eqo writing outside the cavern had spoken of the Icon and the great power it held. It was said to contain the Soul of the Goddess. Claire did not know exactly what that meant, because it had never been mentioned before. There were a few obscure mentions of the Goddess in other places, but this was the first place she had been talked about specifically.

Claire stood there for several minutes, trying to decide what to do. She could continue her work or she could retreat from the cave so she could show her husband. Andrew Donavan was the love of her life and it was only through his personal abilities that she was able to fund this venture. No one had believed her that the Icon existed anymore, if it ever had. She was out here working alone, albeit with the ability to spend each night by her husband's side.

Andrew was a writer and he could therefore work from anywhere. As long as he had electricity to run his computer and either an internet or cellular connection, he was happy. So he continued to work while Claire spent her days excavating the cave, learning everything she could along the way. However, this moment was worth taking him away from his current book so that she could share with him her triumph.

"Fuck it," Claire suddenly said as she reached out just a little more and touched the Icon for the first time. The cold stone would need careful documentation in time, tracing out exactly what it looked like, what it was supposed to represent. From her perspective, it was just a short, round column of stone with line carvings in it. But she had no doubt that this was the lost Icon. She knew it down to her core.

Claire smiled, realizing she was the first human to touch the Icon in thousands of years. No one else had even seen it, let alone touched it since the Eqo people disappeared. She was special. This moment was special.

However, something suddenly happened. Claire found herself flying across the cavern, nearly hitting her head on the rock wall. When she looked up, for the briefest of moments, it looked like the Icon was glowing. But it only lasted for that moment, returning to its cold gray coloration from before. Claire was almost able to write the glowing off as a figment of her imagination, but that did not explain how she had been thrown away from the Icon.

"Was I worthy?" Claire asked herself. She tried to find a reason why she had been tossed across the cavern. She knew it had happened. She was certain she was not crazy. But there was more to this than met the eye. More study was needed.

First, however, Claire needed to see her husband. Andrew would want to hear about her success.

As Claire made her way out of the cave, she wondered if she was wearing the right clothing. Her thick pants, sturdy boots, and woolen sweater was not exactly what one would consider sexy. Not that she was trying to be sexy. She was trying to be comfortable while working in a rocky cave. She made sure to shut off the electricity that ran the lights and the air filtration system upon exiting. There was no sense in wasting precious resources when they were not needed.

It was less than 100 feet to the trailer that served as both their home and Andrew's office while Claire performed her archeology work. She dusted herself off and then opened the door to climb inside.

Andrew was where he always seemed to be. The dining table also served as his office, giving him a platform to work. He had his laptop out and he was happily typing away, writing who knew what. Claire had never particularly cared what he made his money writing. She was always too caught up in her own work to worry about what he was creating. But she had supported his work and he had supported her work, although she had to admit she got more out of the deal than he did. He was paying for the supplies for her to excavate the cave.

"Hi, honey," Claire said. "I've got fantastic news."

Andrew held his finger up for a moment before he went back to typing. He did not say anything, but Claire knew his mannerisms by now. He wanted to finish his thought so that he could give her his undivided attention.

With an emphatic flourish of his hands, he entered a period on his document and then closed the laptop lid. Then he turned to face his wife, smiling to see her so happy and ready to listen to her news.

However, what happened next was unexpected. Claire dropped to her knees and reached for his pants. Before either of them knew what was happening, Claire had freed her husband's cock and began to give him a blowjob. She bobbed her head up and down on his shaft, seemingly reveling in the pleasure she provided him.

This was unusual behavior to say the least. Claire was known to suck her husband's cock on occasion, but not like this. She did not do it in the middle of the day. She did not do it when he was expecting to hear good news from her.

Deep down, Claire recognized that this was strange behavior for her. She could be an odd duck at times, but this went above and beyond anything that she had done before. And yet, she felt completely at ease with this turn of events. More than ever, this felt right. This was what she was supposed to be doing.

As it just so happened, Andrew had just finished writing a particularly sexy scene in his book, so his cock was already hard when Claire came to him. And he was definitely not going to complain about an impromptu blowjob. He was just surprised that her good news came with something else so welcome. He was not a man who would ever turn down sex or a blowjob from the woman he loved.

It was only later, once he had coated Claire's tonsils with his cum and she had swallowed every drop down, even the little rivulet of cum that had escaped the corner of her lips and had been pushed back into her mouth by a finger to suck clean, that

Claire was able to sit back and realize that her behavior was odd.

"That was strange."

"But not unwelcome," Andrew added with a knowing smile.

Claire blushed in response, but she felt the same way. She did not understand why, but she had needed to do that before she could even think of sharing her good news.

"I found it," Claire finally admitted. "I found the lost Icon. It's in the cave. I touched it and it threw me back and then I think it glowed for a moment."

"It threw you back?" Andrew asked, suddenly worried for his wife. Had she hit her head? That did not explain the blowjob, but it might be an explanation for her off behavior.

"I'm okay. I didn't get hurt. But I guess I am feeling a little different. But come. I want to show you the Icon. You won't believe it until you see it."

Claire rose to her feet and pulled Andrew out of his seat. Then she dragged him out of the trailer and into the cave, making sure to turn on the electricity before they entered.

Andrew followed like a dutiful husband, wanting to support his wife. He knew she could be devoted to her work, but he had never seen her this excited about one of her findings before.

Despite him spending many weeks with her out in the middle of nowhere while she excavated the cave, he had not actually entered before. He had kept to himself, mostly in the trailer. And when he needed a break from his book, he would go for hikes around the area. There was no one around for miles, so he was able to enjoy nature in peace. But now that he was seeing all that his wife had been working on, including the massive amount of rock and dirt she had moved by herself, he was more impressed with her dedication than ever.

And before he knew it, they were in the cavern with the Icon. It reminded him a little of the temple in the first Indiana Jones movie. In the middle of the cavern stood a pillar and on that pillar stood the Icon. Or at least he assumed it was the Icon. He never would have known himself, but Claire was convinced and he trusted his wife on such matters. She was the Eqo expert, not him.

"Isn't it beautiful," Claire said. "The Goddess will be so pleased."

Andrew did a double take at his wife's words. They did not make sense to him.

"The Goddess?" He had to ask. He needed confirmation that she was not crazy, because that sounded a little crazy to him. Maybe she had actually hit her head and she did not realize it.

"The Icon is supposed to contain the Soul of the Goddess," Claire explained. "I don't know exactly what that means, since I haven't finished translating all the writings here in the cave. But if I were the Goddess, I would be excited that my Icon had been found. She's no longer lost."

"That's terrific and I'll be sure to help you write your research paper on all of this when you're ready, just as I promised."

"You're the best," Claire said enthusiastically. "And thanks for letting me show you the Icon. I know that you need to work on your book more so I'll let you go. I need to keep translating and documenting my find."

The two parted happily with Claire practically bubbling with excitement. She spent the rest of the day in the cave, working into the evening as she often did. There was so much she still needed to understand. There were writings on the wall that did not make complete sense to her. She needed to think about it more and that kept her working.

However, Claire made several changes to her outfit as she worked, deciding that she did indeed need to look sexier. She did not know why, but it was a compulsion she could not ignore. First, she stripped off the woolen sweater. It was too hot to wear anyway, even though the inside of the cave remained remarkably cool. Then she took a knife to her undershirt, cutting a large swath of fabric away to reveal her midriff. She also cut a deeper neckline to show off what small breasts she did have.

There was nothing Claire could do about the boots she wore. There was no way to make them sexier, but she did manage to turn her pants into shorts. The cuffs were a little uneven, but that was the best she could do until she actually went shopping for proper clothes. Claire did not understand why she was wearing such inappropriate clothing.

When Claire returned to the trailer that night, she paid no attention to the change in her clothing. After a couple hours, she felt completely normal dressed as she was. This was how it was supposed to be. As a woman, she was supposed to be showing off her body.

Andrew would have been more concerned, but that was difficult when a sexy version of his wife walked in the door and wanted to fuck before dinner. He had never known her to be so lustful, but again, he was not going to complain that his wife wanted to have sex with him. And soon enough they were in the back of the trailer, on the bed, Clair on her hands and knees, stripped of her clothes, while Andrew thrust away into her.

Claire screamed out in erotic ecstasy as she came hard. And all the while Andrew kept his cock pistoning in and out of her. She had never been this turned on in all her life. However, the moment she entered the trailer, she knew she needed one thing. She needed her husband's cock in her pussy. And now that she had it there, she could not imagine a better life for herself. She was happy, sexy, and full of cock, just like a woman was supposed to be.

It was only later, after Claire's second orgasm, triggered by Andrew's own orgasm, that she was able to consider how strange those words were. Even then, as she sat there in bed, coming down from the orgasmic high, she knew something was off. Was a woman supposed to be happy, sexy, and full of cock? Sure, those things were nice, but was that how it was supposed to be? She was not so sure.

But Claire's worries disappeared when Andrew brought her a bowl of stew that had been cooking all day. She was hungry and the need for hot food overwhelmed her other considerations. And by the time her food was finished, she found herself drifting off to sleep, completely content with everything that had happened.

However, something had clearly happened to Claire after she touched the Icon. She believed it contained the Soul of the Goddess, whoever the Goddess might be. But that was a slight misinterpretation of the actual meaning. The Icon was an object touched by the Goddess and she had imbued it with some of her power. And that power had now been transferred into Claire. She had been changed. It was her soul specifically. The Icon had swapped out the parts deemed unworthy and replaced them with parts that were approved.

So little was known about the Eqo people that it was easy to misinterpret their art and writings. Eqo society was structured patriarchally to an extreme degree. Women were raised to be a certain way. They performed very specific functions in society and they were expected to look a certain way. Beauty was coveted over brains and the more beautiful a woman was, their minds were usually the slowest. That was how life was. Women were bimbos and the men focused on advancing society.

And for those women who were troubled by all of this, there was a solution. The Icon, containing the essence of the Goddess, was used to bring them into line. Had Claire spent more time studying the writings of the people she studied and less time obsessing over the lost Icon, she might have figured this out before it was too late.

That night, as she slept beside her husband, Claire began to transform. She had brought the essence of the Goddess into her soul and now that her soul had become perfect in the eyes of the Eqo people, she needed to become perfect in the same way.

Had Andrew been awake throughout all of this, he would have watched as Claire's hair lightened in color. This was not strictly necessary, but the essence of the Goddess that had attached itself to Claire's soul could look into her mind to better understand what was now considered to be fashionable. It understood how much time had passed since the last time it had helped a woman become their best self. The rules were the same, but there were subtle differences that could not be ignored. And lighter hair was considered better in Claire's case.

But beneath the covers was where the major changes took place. Claire's whole body began to transform, her midriff tightening as the extraneous fat shifted to her ass, making it bigger and rounder. Most noticeable were the growth of her tits. They ballooned off of her chest, gaining in mass far faster than should have been possible. Ancient magic turned her entire body into an erotic playground as she slept, doing what would have needed years and significant money spent on doctors and surgeons to complete in only a few hours.

When Claire woke up the next morning, there was a dopey smile on her face. It took her a moment to fully process that she was awake and that her husband was beside her. Then without even thinking, she dove beneath the bedding to find his morning wood.

In some ways, her blowjob was a repeat of the one she had given him before telling him of her fantastic news. Only this time there were a few differences. One, Claire could easily take Andrew's cock into her throat now, her gag reflex disappearing overnight. Two, her lips had plumped up overnight and were now perfectly designed to wrap around a big cock and provide it with maximum pleasure. She had been completely remade for this and so much more.

"Fuck me," Andrew groaned as he woke up to find his cock

enveloped in his wife's mouth. He opened his eyes to see her bubble butt sticking out from underneath the covers, but it took him several moments to realize that she looked different, even from that angle.

Not that Andrew was complaining. Deep down, there were things he had wished were different about his wife. Her being generally hotter was high on the list. He wanted to see her with a bigger ass, bigger tits, and all the other little things that went with that.

Had Andrew been honest with himself, he would have known that he wished Claire had been a bimbo. He loved the look and he did have a thing for dumb women who needed a man's guidance. That had always turned him on, but he had long ago figured it was not to be. He had settled. That was not to say he disliked Claire as she was. He loved her. He cared about her. He only wished that she was more for him.

And now she was, although not because of anything he had done.

Claire made quick work of the wake-up blowjob. She felt like an expert when it came to cock now. It was something she was proud about. When her head popped up from underneath the covers, she had the same dopey smile on her face. Andrew laid there, still covered, stunned by the transformation his wife had undergone overnight. He knew it was her. He could still recognize her, although there were some significant differences. The basics were still the same.

But it was Claire's eyes that told the real story. They looked the same. They were the same color. They were Claire's eyes. But as they say, the eyes are windows into the soul. And that soul was now on complete display. Andrew now understood what had happened, even if he did not understand why. Claire's soul had been changed. Parts of her had been swapped out and replaced with better parts.

There was no doubt that Claire was a bimbo now. Even if

she had some small hope of retaining her intelligence, making her first activity upon waking be a blowjob sealed her fate. There was no hope in resurrecting her archeology career. Her skills were best suited for other endeavors now, ones that were aided by a sexy body with big tits and a big ass, and that did not require much in the way of intellectual thought.

"I guess we won't need to worry about writing that paper now," Andrew joked, but Claire simply smiled, not knowing how to respond to his statement.

Claire was still there, or some version of her was still there. But her body screamed at her, wanting her attention. It wanted sex and with her diminished mind, she could not hold back against her body's demands.

"Let's get started with the day," Andrew announced.

"Okay, hubby," Claire answered as she jumped off the bed, rocking the trailer a little with her sudden movements, before she hurried off to make herself look properly presentable. A recently awake bimbo could be hot, but she wanted to make sure she met the day with her best face forward and that meant washing and generally making herself look as sexy as possible.

Having a feeling that Claire would be a while, Andrew wrapped a robe around himself and slipped on a pair of shoes. He had some investigations of his own to make. He turned on the electric lights and air pump on his way into the cave. He carried his phone with him and fully intended to document everything that he could. The cave looked just as it had when Claire had shown him it the day before. But now he looked at everything with a greater understanding, as well as far more questions.

Andrew realized that it was now up to him to finish his wife's work. He had just picked up two new hobbies to work on in addition to his writing schedule. There was figuring out how the Icon had transformed his wife, which he was more than happy about, but also keeping his wife's enhanced libido satisfied. Luckily, he could at least set her to work at sucking his cock while he worked. That would keep her busy part of the time and allow him to work as well, albeit at a slower rate.

Andrew took pictures of everything he could think of. Every surface was recorded for later analysis. And when it came time to deal with the Icon itself, Andrew hesitated before he reached out to touch it, much like Claire had the day before. But when his fingers finally made contact with the cold stone, nothing happened. The Icon was primed to work with women, not men. As a man, Andrew was completely ignored by the magic and the essence of the Goddess within.

And since Andrew was safe to touch the Icon, he scooped it up off the pillar and carried it back to the trailer. It was time to go home. Claire had done what she had come to this spot to do. She had found the lost Icon of the Eqo and in the process she had transformed herself, turning into a bimbo with the magic of the past civilization.

When Andrew returned to the trailer, he found Claire sitting at the table, eating a bowl of cereal. At least she could still take care of herself. She was not completely useless. She had not been turned into a human doll. However, there was now no question at how much she had changed. Her choice of clothing was a testament to her transformed outlook on life.

Before all of this started for her, Claire had made sure to bring a few sexy outfits with her. Spending all this time out with her husband required some fun. They did not leave a monastic life. So that meant she had a little bit of lingerie to wear. The pink thong still fit, since it did not have to stretch over her ass, just around it. The matching bra had no hope of fitting, but Claire did not seem to mind. And her bigger tits were perky and firm, despite their rapid growth and much larger size.

The sheer white dress Claire wore, however, was what made her new intentions clear. Everything was visible through the transparent material. That was how Andrew knew she wore her pink thong. He could see it through her dress. But she wore nothing else underneath it, leaving her big tits and her hard nipples on full display. Andrew realized he would need to take her shopping, but seeing her in that outfit and how sexy she looked, he was going to enjoy his wife looking like a complete sexpot for as long as he could get away with it.

It was only after he had taken in her outfit, paying special attention to her tits, as they were prominently displayed in that dress as it struggled to contain her new curves, that Andrew noticed her heels. She had found her one pair of high heels that she had brought with her on this adventure, a pair of kitten heels that admittedly perfectly matched the dress. Claire was a vision in pink and white and he could not wait to unwrap her later and give his bimbo a proper fucking.

However, there was something he needed to do first. He needed to talk to her.

"Claire, honey, do you understand what happened to you?" Andrew asked as he sat down across from her at the table. He noticed how she had left him his usual work space open to him, choosing to sit across from where he had spent hours typing away on his laptop.

"I turned into a bimbo, right?" Claire answered. Even her voice had risen an octave or so, giving her the perfect voice to match her bimbo body.

"That's right. Do you know why?"

Claire sat there and thought about it for a long time. He was glad to see that she did not immediately dismiss the questions and shake her head. There was still a brain in that head of hers, although it was clear it had been retested for different purposes.

"This is how the Goddess wants me to be," Claire finally answered. "Women are supposed to be bimbos. I wasn't before, but the Goddess made me better."

Andrew nodded his head, using this information to put the final pieces together. There was still much that he did not understand, but he was certain that between the pictures he took, the Icon itself, and what remained of Claire's mind, he could figure it out. If only he did not have a writing deadline to meet, he would devote all of his time to figuring out this mystery.

Well, not all of his time. There was no way he was going to pass up fucking his bimbo in each and every way that he could think of. And as a man who had written a lot of sex scenes in his life, he had a lot of ideas on that subject.

As for Claire, she was happy. Her brain was constantly awash with endorphins. She was rewarded by the Goddess for every sexy action she took, which only served to further push her over the edge into bimbodom. She had a sexy body, a raging libido, a simplified mind, and the emotional range of a teaspoon, but she was happy. She had achieved her life's work and then gotten the chance to live a whole new life with meaning. And lots and lots of sex. That last part could not be forgotten.

And as soon as Claire was done with her breakfast, Andrew took her back to bed so that he could give her a proper bimbo fucking. She deserved it as far as he was concerned. And with her sexy body swaying around, his cock needed it. This was their new life.

2

THE MESSAGE

Sonja dismounted her motorcycle and stepped up toward the home of her best friend going all the way back to college. It had been a difficult few months for the now former librarian. It seemed that each month something new and horrible happened to her and it had really started to wear her down.

It all started when Claire left with her husband for an expedition to research the Eqo people. Sonja loved that her friend was so excited about her work, willing to put her own money into an expedition that no university even considered funding. However, it meant Sonja had gone without her best friend for all that time, taking away the natural support network that the pair had for each other since their university days.

After that, Sonja's car got stolen and completely destroyed in a joyride situation. Insurance blamed her, believing that she had been the one to destroy her car and not the car thieves. Sonja was certain she would eventually get the money for the car, but in the meantime she had to fight the insurance company. Luckily, she still had her motorcycle.

Then there was the breakup with her boyfriend. In the big

picture, breaking up was for the best. Sonja and Edward were not right for each other, but it was just bad timing and it was another support structure that had been pulled out from under her.

The last straw had been losing her job at the library. Budget cuts were hitting hard after a bond levy failed to pass. The library tried to keep Sonja on for as long as they could, but at a certain point it came down to cutting staff or cutting back on the books the library carried. Sonja could not blame the choice being made, but it meant she was out of a job and facing eviction if she could not come up with next month's rent.

At least Claire was back. That was the one bright spot for the out of work librarian. She had her friend back.

Not that Claire had been forthcoming about her return. Sonja had heard nothing from her friend, not knowing she was back in town. It was actually seeing Andrew, Claire's husband, at the grocery store that helped Sonja reconnect with her friend.

However, the few text messages they had sent each other made it clear that something had changed. Sonja was not sure if it was something that had changed in their relationship or if it was Claire herself who had changed. It was impossible to be certain via text message.

Apparently it had been Andrew's idea to invite Sonja over. That was the general impression Sonja had received from the invitation. Not that Sonja was willing to turn down an invitation to see her best friend. She just did not understand what had changed between them.

Sonja walked up the front steps and rang the doorbell. She was dressed in jeans and a leather jacket. She held her motorcycle helmet in her arms as she waited. Sonja was sure her hair was a little rumpled. The helmet had a tendency to do that, but the motorcycle was her only mode of transportation until the situation with the insurance company played out. And that assumed she finally won. The fact her lawyer was not getting paid was a problem. She was afraid he would drop her case, since she could no longer afford his services.

The door opened and Andrew greeted her. "Welcome, Sonja. I'm glad you could make it. Please, come in."

Andrew beckoned Sonja inside the house and she immediately felt as if she were walking into a stranger's house. She had visited Claire here many times before. She had visited for dinner with both Claire and Andrew as well. But there was something very different about the house now than she remembered.

Yes, Sonja knew that Andrew and Claire had been gone for several months, leaving their house empty while Claire was out hunting for clues about the Eqo people. But the house did not look as if it had sat empty for all that time. It also did not look fully lived in either. There were no piles of books on every flat surface. Claire was known to be someone who created a lot of piles. Even the dining room table would have piles when she was invited over to eat, each corner either covered in a stack of books or a pile of papers.

The house looked clean and smelled fresher than Sonja could remember it ever being before. It did not make sense. Nothing made sense. And there was no sign of Claire. It was like she was hiding. Or maybe she actually refused to be friends with Sonja anymore and was not even in the house. Maybe this was just Andrew trying to smooth things over and it blowing up in his face.

"Claire is still getting ready," Andrew explained. "She's very excited to meet you, but she wanted me to explain a few things before she came out to greet you."

Sonja simply nodded her head, not fully understanding what Andrew could mean, although she was relieved to hear that Claire was excited. She only wished Claire had been able to express that to her. Instead, Sonja had been left to worry that

Claire no longer wanted to be friends, which given her situation, would have completely destroyed her.

"Let's take a seat," Andrew said, motioning toward the living room couches. Sonja placed her helmet on a side table and took a seat, sinking into the soft cushions. There was a warmth on the couch that she could not fully understand, but it was comfortable and that was what mattered.

"This is all very confusing," Sonja eventually said once she got herself comfortable. She shrugged off her leather jacket, revealing the black top beneath. But she kept the jacket with her. Sonja had a tendency to get cold and she always kept her jacket or coat with her, regardless of the situation. "Claire has sounded strange in her messages."

Andrew sat down across from his wife's friend. He had been trying to figure out what to say to her since he had made the invitation to her. The trouble was, he had a hard time deciding how to share the fact that his wife and Sonja's best friend was now a bimbo. That was not something that seemed acceptable, let alone normal. Yes, Andrew had learned that a few women had turned themselves into bimbos on their own. Others were bimbos more naturally.

However, this was a case of an ancient artifact that had possessed or traded out parts of Claire's soul, transforming her from the inside out. It should not have been possible, but the proof was currently finishing putting on her makeup, nearly ready to come join the party, so to speak.

"Claire changed a lot recently," Andrew tried to explain. "She found the missing Icon she was looking for, but the sculpture holds some sort of mystical or magic power."

Sonja naturally scoffed at Andrew's description. She was a librarian and understood there was a difference between reality and the religious beliefs of ancient people. The Eqo people may have believed their Icon held mystical powers, but it did not really. Magic and true mysticism did not exist.

"She touched the Icon and over the course of the next day or so, Claire turned into a bimbo."

As if a cue had been given, the clickety-clack of high heels sounded Claire's approach. Sonja turned to watch as a blonde-haired vision of bimbolicious proportions appeared in the doorway to the living room. Sonja's jaw nearly hit the floor at the sight of her friend, all gussied up in a tight minidress that emphasized every one of Claire's impressive curves and high-lighted her big tits, narrow waist, wide hips, and long legs.

"Hi, Sonja," Claire cooed, followed by a giggle. She sashayed across the room and leaned over, bending at the waist, to give her friend a hug.

Sonja could only stare as she got an eyeful of cleavage, some-thing Claire had never had before. It seemed as if the once smart and capable woman that Sonja had known for all these years was no more. In her place was a cooing bimbo with hardly a thought in her head.

Claire's hug was returned, but Sonja looked awkward as she wrapped her arms around her friend. She was afraid of touching Claire somewhere inappropriate. Little did she realize that no part of Claire's body was considered off limits or inap-propriate anymore. She was an over-sexed bimbo and would have happily walked outside in the nude, only wearing a pair of high heels, if Andrew allowed her. He had realized he needed to keep his wife on a short leash to prevent such mishaps.

"I don't understand," Sonja finally said once Claire broke the embrace and then sat down beside her husband, pressing her nubile body into his. Her long-nailed hand rested on his thigh, but Sonja could guess that her hand would slowly drift toward Andrew's crotch as the conversation continued.

Andrew went on to explain exactly what had happened. He left out no details, including sharing about the first moment he became suspicious, when Claire had given him an impromptu blowjob. Claire said nothing, but she made a purring noise as

Andrew described some of the more sexual acts they got up to after Claire touched the Icon.

Normally, Sonja would have thought this all fiction. But the proof was right in front of her. There was no other way she could explain Claire's transformation. Sure, she supposed this could have all been an elaborate ruse, the expedition really a chance for Claire to go off and get surgery, blowing up her tits and everything else, including the recovery time, but that did not sound like her friend. This was not the woman Sonja had gone to college with. It was like all of her knowledge had been emptied out of her head to make room for anything and everything sexual related.

"Wow," Sonja finally said as everything finally started to sink in. It had really happened. Magic or mysticism or whatever it was turned out to be real. "Am I the first person you've shared this with?"

Andrew nodded his head. He looked far more comfortable now. Then again, Claire's hand had indeed slid toward his crotch and she gently massaged his cock through his pants. Sonja could only guess that he had become accustomed to Claire's hand resting there and had come to expect it from her.

"I'll admit, we're both still adjusting to this new life, but I figured as Claire's best friend, you should be the one to hear about this first, seeing the new her. I'd hate to see the two of you run into each other somewhere and let it turn into a big scene."

This time it was Sonja who nodded. She could imagine just that. Claire would be out shopping somewhere, maybe buying groceries, although it was unclear if she was capable of such things now. She seemed to be rather limited beyond just looking amazingly hot. But even with all the changes to her mind and body, it was still clearly Claire. And then it would be Sonja who freaked out, causing a scene. Claire might actually enjoy the extra attention, but that would only drive Sonja even more into a frenzy. No, it had been smart to set up this dinner. Sonja needed a chance to see the new Claire in a private setting.

"Claire, are you happy?" It was the one question that really mattered and Sonja needed the answer. As long as her friend was happy, Sonja would accept this new wrinkle in their friendship. She did not even know if remaining friends was possible anymore. They had so little in common anymore.

"Being a bimbo is the best," Claire said, her voice melodious and higher pitched than the way she spoke before the transformation. "I wish you could be a bimbo too."

Sonja's first reaction was to scoff at the mere thought of becoming what Claire had been turned into. She was a librarian. She loved books and knowledge and she did not care about things like fashion or style. However, Sonja could not deny that her friend was happy. And it was not exactly like Sonja was in a happy place right then. She was near rock bottom and seeing her friend like this only made it worse. Her friend could sympathize, but she could not truly understand Sonja's pain.

Their friendship had been altered in ways that would make it difficult to survive. Claire was a bimbo and Sonja was not.

"I'm gonna go get the statue thingy," Claire announced as she jumped up from the couch, her big tits bouncing in her tight dress, barely able to stop the massive motion on her chest.

It looked like Andrew might try to stop her, but even he realized it was difficult to argue with a bimbo. Yes, she viewed him as an authority figure, but Claire's mind was so simple that once she got fixated on something, it was difficult to get her to stop. Andrew would have had to be his most commanding and he did not see the point. After all, Claire was only moving up his original plans, not actually going against them.

Claire was only gone for a minute. After mincing out of the room, she returned holding the small Eqo sculpture. Sonja was no expert, but she immediately recognized some of the markings on the sculpture as distinctly Eqo in origin. Claire had shared enough of her research for Sonja to pick up on it all.

"Don't touch it," Andrew called out as it looked like Claire was about to hand the sculpture to her friend.

Sonja immediately pulled her hands back, realizing that there could have been a huge mistake. If the Icon could turn Claire into a bimbo, what would it do to her?

Claire pouted, but it only lasted for a moment. She was displeased that Sonja did not automatically turn herself into a bimbo too, but she quickly got over it. It was all but impossible for Claire to stay upset for long. Her bimbofied brain kept her on a steady dose of endorphins and other pleasurable hormones. There was just too much fun to be had as a bimbo for her to remain upset for very long.

"Put the Icon on the coffee table," Andrew said, his voice sounding like an order.

And then without a word, Claire did exactly as she was told. It was almost an unthinking action. She did it without any conscious thought of her own, her body responding without direct input from her brain.

Sonja was partially horrified at her friend's behavior. This was not the Claire that she had once known. Although she had to also admit that Claire seemed far more happy than she ever had before. It seemed that all of that thinking had gotten in the way of her happiness. Then again, Claire had fulfilled her long dream of finding the Icon, so she had reason to be satisfied with her previous life. It was just that now she found satisfaction in another style of living, one that more often saw Claire on her knees before her husband instead of in a cave.

Once the Icon was safely on the table, Claire returned to her spot beside her husband, pressing her voluptuous body up against him. She looked perfectly content sitting there, especially once her hand once again returned to her husband's crotch. She took great comfort from being close to him, knowing that he would protect her and provide for her as long as she gave herself to him fully. She was by no means a trophy wife, but she was as close as could conceivably come to that moniker.

"So life is good for the two of you?" Sonja asked. It seemed obvious, but appearances could be deceiving. And besides, it was more a question for Andrew. She was pretty sure what Claire would say. She looked completely blissful, without a care in the world.

"It's taken some adjustments, but yes, I think we've found a good place for ourselves. And my writing output has never been better. Claire knows how to motivate me."

Claire did not say anything. Instead, she nibbled gently on Andrew's ear, clearly wanting to take things further, but knowing that she could not while they had company. Sonja had never seen anyone so sexual in her life. She had no idea it was even possible. And to see it from the woman she had once called her best friend was both disconcerting and oddly exciting. She was happy for her friend, while at the same time she was worried for her.

As Sonja sat there, trying not to watch her friend get engrossed by the thought of fucking her husband, which was what Claire clearly wanted, she found herself instead looking at the sculpture on the coffee table between them. It was strange, because Sonja felt as if the Icon was calling to her. She felt a pull towards it that she could not explain. It was almost as if there were whispers in her ears, but she could not make out the words.

"Is everything all right?" Andrew asked. Sonja glanced up to see concern etched in the lines of his face. But she only glanced up for a moment, because her gaze was drawn right back down to the stone sculpture again. She simply could not stand to look away for long.

"Everything is fine," Sonja commented, her voice sounding far away as she heard herself speak.

And it was all fine. Yes, Sonja was faced with an overwhelming burden ahead of her. She needed to look for a new job. She needed to deal with the lawyers. She needed to keep herself from getting evicted. But somehow, she felt as if the Icon held an answer for her. It felt as if it was telling her that it could make all her problems go away. She just needed to reach out and touch it. Then she could live her happiest and best life with a purpose she never had before.

It was a tempting offer. Very tempting.

The problem was, Sonja could not think of a good reason not to try touching the Icon. Sure, maybe her mind was being manipulated. She certainly felt a pull toward the sculpture, a desire to touch it that felt unnatural. And yet, it felt completely natural at the same time. What woman would not give up her intelligence and independence so that she could be a bimbo? Sure, the logic was not there, but that did not stop the desire from forming deep inside the former librarian.

And just like that, Sonja made her decision. It definitely was not rational, but rationality was unimportant compared to the broader realization that she was meant to touch the Icon. It was almost required of her.

"What are you doing?" Andrew asked, both surprised and worried as he watched Sonja lean forward.

Claire simply giggled, somehow understanding what Sonja was doing. Then again, she had experienced the same pull, although in a completely different way.

Sonja did not answer. Her gaze was locked onto the Icon. She did not even register Andrew's question or Claire's giggling. Her entire world had narrowed down to the small sculpture. Nothing else mattered.

The moment Sonja's fingers touched the cool stone, she felt a shock travel up her arm and straight into her head. Unlike

Claire, who was rocketed away from the Icon and nearly hit the wall of the cave where she had found the sculpture, Sonja's fingers became stuck. She could not pull away even if she wanted to. New information was being uploaded into her mind, her future, both as a bimbo and for the purpose she would fulfill.

Andrew could only sit and watch as Sonja's soul was examined by the Icon and parts of her replaced. He had a rough idea of what she might be going through, after hearing Claire explain it, although her transformation into a bimbo made such explanations now impossible. Nonetheless, he understood that Sonja was getting measured by the mystic Goddess that lived on in the lost Icon of the Eqo. And whatever parts of her that were found wanting would be replaced by that same goddess.

Time lost all meaning for Sonja as she sat there, her hand outstretched and her fingers touching the stone. When the upload finally finished, she retracted her hand and blinked rapidly, trying to process what had just happened.

When Sonja's mouth opened, she began to speak as if she was controlled by some other force. "I bring a message to the people of this world. The Goddess will return in full force. We must find her a vessel. That is my purpose."

Then Sonja blinked rapidly and she seemed to return to herself. Only, this time when she looked at Andrew and Claire sitting across from her, she smiled and licked her lips. Somehow she knew life was about to get a lot more interesting.

After that, the evening went much more normally. Andrew ushered Claire and Sonja into the dining room so that they could eat dinner. He had already prepared most of the meal. It just needed the final touches.

Although normal was a bit of an overstatement. Claire started her dinner underneath the table, between Andrew's legs. Sonja would have been horrified about what her friend was doing before all of this. Now, she almost felt like it was expected. And more than that, she found the whole concept turned her on.

Sonja bit her lip between bites of food as she listened to Claire sucking away on Andrew's cock. Andrew focused on eating, although he was not fully successful, his face turning red as he had never had anyone watch this new dinner time routine. That was until Claire's work overwhelmed Andrew's pleasure centers and he was no longer able to feel shame under the great onslaught of his oncoming orgasm. And by then Sonja was too turned on to care.

The only person who showed no hint of anything was Claire. Once she was done, once she had swallowed down all of Andrew's cum, she crawled out from under the table and returned to her seat. She did not even look flustered before she began to eat her meal.

For the most part, the trio ate in silence. What more was there to say? Claire babbled occasionally, but whatever the Icon had in store for Sonja was only just beginning. And Claire's mostly incomprehensible words simply did not provide for lively dinner conversation.

However, by the time Sonja had finished eating, there was one truth she simply could no longer deny. She was horny. She was really fucking horny. And even more, her mouth was watering for cock.

Sonja was no stranger to blowjobs, but she had always reserved them for special occasions. Of course, without a boyfriend any longer, it was not like she was just going to go out and suck off a random man in the bathroom of a bar. She still had standards, even if they had significantly changed in the past hour.

"I think it's my turn," Sonja suddenly announced. She got up from her seat at the table and walked past Claire. She whispered something in her friend's ear, but Andrew could not hear it.

However, Claire nodded eagerly, giggling at whatever Sonja had suggested.

"Andrew, Claire got to suck your cock at the start of dinner," Sonja announced as she stood beside him. "I think I should get to suck your cock after dinner."

Andrew looked from Sonja to Claire, questioning whether all of this was possible. But Claire seemed genuinely excited to have Sonja give her husband a blowjob. It was only then dawning on him that he was about to have two bimbos at his beck and call. The possibilities were certainly going to be more fun.

"Get to work," Andrew said, pushing himself back slightly from the table to give Sonja more room.

Not missing a beat, Sonja dropped to her knees and crawled under the table. She used deft fingers to free Andrew's cock. Even though it had not been that long since Claire's blowjob, his cock was hard, not at all minding the idea of having two girls serve him instead of just one.

And the moment Sonja wrapped her lips around Andrew's cock, she was in heaven. It felt as if her whole world was finally coming into alignment. This was how life was supposed to be. She was not supposed to be a librarian. She was not supposed to be an independent woman. She was supposed to be a dumb bimbo serving a smart man. It all made so much more sense.

As the happiness bubbled up out of Sonja's bimbofied soul, she realized that despite her soon to be dim intelligence and whatever upgrades her body received, she still had a mission to complete. She had been given a message. She had a purpose that was more than just serving a man like Andrew with her body. She needed to find the perfect vessel so that the Goddess could be reborn. Not that she knew who she was looking for. She did not even know what qualities she would need to look for. But her purpose was clear. The Goddess needed her and demanded her service.

Sonja's blowjob lasted longer than Claire's had, but that had more to do with the time between orgasms than it had on Sonja's skill. Claire was still the superior cocksucker, but that was mostly because her lips and mouth had transformed for that purpose. Plump lips and a dexterous tongue helped drive Andrew to orgasm faster, no matter what technique was used.

"I guess that means you'll be spending the night," Andrew offered. "And you'll probably be moving in. When you're fully bimbofied, I think I'm going to have to set you two up on one of those fan sites so you can make some money."

Claire clapped and bounced in her seat, excited at the idea. She did not really know what her husband was talking about, but she was certain it would be fun, especially because she would be doing it with her bimbofied friend. Sonja was still kneeling at Andrew's feet, still with her head beneath the table, savoring the last remnants of Andrew's cum on her tongue. However, she had to agree that Andrew made a lot of sense. Why worry about a real job when she and Claire could just be sexy bimbos together on camera? She was certain men would pay for that.

For the rest of the night, Andrew and Sonja planned. They needed to unwind her past life before the bimbofication fully took her mind from her. Claire was useless in almost all matters now. However, she had other uses. As the two plotted, Claire alternated between acting as a cock sleeve for husband and licking Sonja's pussy. Thankfully, Sonja had everything she needed on her phone. She might not be able to contact the various people she needed to contact, so she handed that information over to Andrew.

There was nothing official signed, but Andrew and Sonja agreed that he would act as her power of attorney. He would control her finances and arrange for her possessions to be moved to the house or sold off, depending on what was best. They were both expecting Sonja to be fully bimbofied by morning. That was what happened to Claire. She went from archeologist to bimbo in less than a day. The whole transformation was impressive.

"We should record me while I sleep tonight, just to see what happens," Sonja suggested.

"I'll get the video camera. If I can't record the whole night, I can set it for time lapse photography."

It took hours to get everything ironed out, but once they did, the real fun could happen.

Sonja was not thrilled with sharing Andrew with Claire at the start. It was not so much the sharing, but the activity participating in a two girls, one guy sex party. There was still too much of the old Sonja inside, even if she had felt the desire to for sex. Not that she stopped Andrew and Claire from partaking. One look in Claire's eyes and Sonja knew there was no stopping the bimbo. If she did not get fucked by her husband, she would go crazy. And a crazy bimbo was not something Sonja wanted to see.

And so rather than participate, Sonja watched and masturbated. She sat to the side, in an armchair Andrew brought into the bedroom. She played with her pussy and clit, driving herself wild as she also worked and kneaded her breasts. She sat there, completely nude, her legs splayed apart and draped over the chair arms. It was the first time she had ever masturbated to a live personal porn show and she loved it.

But it was the view of Claire, on her hands and knees, getting fucked from behind by her husband that provided the main source of Sonja's arousal. Claire was facing her, but the bimbo's eyes were closed, her face lost in an expression of pure erotic bliss. She moaned with each and every hard thrust, her tits swaying beneath her as her body was pummeled by Andrew's cock.

"Holy fuck, that's hot," Sonja moaned, adding her own noise to the chorus of sex. Her fingers danced as she imagined herself in Claire's place, her body gaining the exaggerated curves of a bimbo, complete with the big tits, the plump lips, and the blissfully ignorant expression on her face, unable to understand even simple concepts that did not relate to sex and fashion.

Sonja quickly found herself on the verge of cumming, but she managed to hold herself back. She stayed right on the edge, keeping herself primed for the big moment. And she sat there on the edge for a long time, continuing to rub and play, waiting for the big moment when Andrew and Claire came.

However, that took a long time. Both Andrew and Claire were now well experienced in their debauchery, able to prolong each other's pleasure for extended periods of time, making the most of the time they spent together. Sonja could only hope that she someday had that level of control. She could manage with her fingers alone, but if there was another cock involved, she doubted she would be able to stop herself from cumming all over it.

In a miraculous turn of fate, all three came together. Andrew's cock surged with another hot load of cum, filling his wife's pussy as he held himself inside of her. Claire was cumming too, her arms giving out as a cascading wave of pleasure flowed through her and her orgasmic screams getting muffled by the bed covers beneath her. And then there was Sonja. There was nothing to stop her from screaming out in orgasmic ecstasy as her first post-Icon climax rushed through her. Her whole body became flush as previously unknown pleasure permeated every fiber of her body.

It was unlike anything Sonja had ever experienced before. The orgasm rushed through her like a freight train, redefining what it meant to feel pleasure, to cum. Every other sexual activity from her past paled in comparison. Her ex-boyfriend was forgotten, his memory unable to live up to her new reality. Sonja was stunned and excited for the journey she was now embarking on.

"Come join us," Andrew beckoned once they had all finished. Claire and Sonja remained nude, but Andrew had thrown on a shirt and a pair of shorts, more for his own comfort than any sense of modesty. Considering what Sonja had already witnessed, Andrew was not concerned about modesty.

Claire and Andrew had an extra big king bed. Sonja found herself snuggling up next to him with Claire pressed to his other side. Even if Claire and Sonja were not on bimbo journeys, Andrew would have been considered a lucky man. But now it felt better than luck.

Sonja admitted it was awkward to know that there was a camera rolling with her in the center of the frame. Lights had been left on so that her transformation could be documented. But that awkwardness soon faded as sleep pulled her down, letting the magic happen while she slept.

And what magic it was. The camera caught everything. Top of the list was Sonja's impressive breast growth. Her small boobs that barely required a bra before, ballooned off her chest as if they were being filled with air. However, they were far heavier than that, although it was difficult to know that by just looking. And what the camera failed to catch was how Sonja's back muscles strengthened to compensate for the added weight on her chest. Her big tits would never cause her any pain.

Also invisible to the camera was the way Sonja's ass filled out into a proper bubble butt. It could only record the slight lifting of her hips, but that was partially hidden by the expansion of her hips, further exaggerating her hourglass figure. Her three holes also transformed, although in far more subtle ways, with her throat losing its gag reflex and the tightening of her vocal cords that would forever raise the pitch of her voice. Her pussy gained muscle dexterity to better milk a cock inside of her. And finally her ass gained similar control, not to mention an increase in pleasure inducing nerves to make getting fucked in the ass a much more pleasurable experience.

Sonja was already well on her way to becoming a three hole bimbo slut.

The camera did catch how her feet became more pointed throughout the night, her tendons transforming to keep her on her toes. It also captured the lightening and lengthening of her hair. By the time the night was through, the once brunette librarian had turned into a blonde with voluminous wavy hair. Unfortunately, Sonja's new hair got in the way of a clear view of her lips plumping up. But they eventually came back into view by the end, Sonja's head shifting in her sleep, showing off the thick pleasure pillows clearly serving only one purpose.

The final change could not be seen by the camera, but the video recording would provide subtle clues to it happening. As the night progressed, Sonja's expression slowly shifted in her sleep. Where once it had been stern, even in her sleeping form, her expression softened slowly through the night until the smallest hint of a smile appeared on her face. This was not in reaction to any dream—although her dreams were erotic and fun to the point she nearly came in her sleep—but a general change in her disposition with her thoughts and worries disappearing.

When Sonja's eyes fluttered open at the sound of her friends stirring, her smile broadened, feeling a completeness that had always been lacking before. Her mind drifted aimlessly for a while as she adjusted to her newly bimbofied existence. No longer burdened by worries or the need to understand the world, Sonja remained blissfully blank, simply happy to feel hot and sexy.

However, once she heard the male groan of Andrew laying next to her, Sonja's mind snapped to attention. She was in bed with a man. No, it was better than that. She was in bed with a man and her best friend. The possibilities were endless.

Sonja sat up and discovered Claire was doing the exact same thing.

"You're so hot now," Claire squealed. She immediately reached out and started feeling up Sonja's new tits. The new bimbo moaned as her arousal spiked. Her tits had never felt that good before. Claire's hands had her seeing stars as her tongue hung out of her mouth, panting in response to her friend's uninvited, but very much appreciated, groping.

"Fuck me," Andrew groaned with pleasure as he opened his eyes to see his wife and her best friend playing with each other with him in the middle.

"Okay," Sonja said, not realizing that Andrew had not meant it literally. He had not meant for her to climb on top of him and ride his morning wood. He had just been expressing his amazement at the sight he woke up to, but he certainly did not mind at all as Sonja's velvety folds enveloped his manhood.

Sonja's eyes turned glassy as the pleasure of being filled pushed away in remaining thoughts. She became a creature of instinct, acting fully through natural intuition, the intuition of a bimbo to provide maximum pleasure to her partner while at the same time maximizing her own pleasure.

Andrew's hands automatically reached up and began to play with Sonja's new tits. That only made her eyes lose even more focus. But it was Claire who completed the threesome. Not to be outdone, she turned the opposite direction and straddled her husband's face, letting him have at her fold with his tongue. Andrew was an equal opportunity man and knew that if Claire was going to suck his cock, it was only fair that he eat her out when she desired. And there was no way he was going to leave her out of the morning fuck-fest.

Soon the two bimbos were making out as they each got fucked by Andrew. Sonja lacked some of the bimbo experience Claire had gained, so she was primarily a recipient of Claire's kisses, but she still managed to buck and grind her hips against the man the two bimbos now shared.

Sonja had never felt anything like this before. Her whole

body hummed with erotic pleasure, her arousal higher than it had ever been before. She had been turned into pure sex and it was amazing. Her body just acted, with little conscious thought from her mind. Instead, she just gave in and let herself live in the moment, enjoying every touch, every shift of the cock inside of her, every wet kiss from her best friend. It was all so great. She was wet and ready and enjoying her newly bimbofied existence.

But this moment of morning sexual bliss was not a simple act of threesome love making. It was not two bimbos riding their man. It all quickly evolved into a table of limbs as Andrew, Claire, and Sonja fucked each other in every way imaginable. Sonja licked pussy, she sucked cock, she got fucked in the pussy, and she got fucked in the ass. She even had Andrew's cock between her big bimbo tits.

And the orgasms were more than she could ever have asked for. She and Claire were cumming over and over again, their bodies filled to the brim with orgasmic pleasure. It got to the point where Sonja could not be sure when one orgasm ended and the next one began. The trio played for hours, each of them enjoying themselves and the pleasure they received, while also proud about the pleasure they were able to provide for each other.

When Andrew finally came onto Sonja and Claire's tits, thick ropes of cum shooting across their skin, giving the two bimbos even more reason to lick each other clean, the three-some finally reduced to a duo.

And once Claire and Sonja had cleaned each other with their tongues, they continued their fun in the shower, making doubly sure that they were both clean for the true start of their day. Not that either of them were able to go the whole shower without adding to the total sum of their morning orgasms. Even had Sonja been able to count that high anymore, she would have easily lost track of how many times she had cum. But it had to have been a record for her, not just in terms of the most orgasms in a day, but likely doubling her lifelong total.

"This was so much fun," Sonja said once they were both out of the shower. They both enjoyed using soft, fluffy towels to dry each other off. Sonja may or may not have cum again, but she was not even paying attention to that anymore. Instead, she had only one thought running through her mind. "But I need to go look for the vessel for the Goddess."

Claire absentmindedly nodded her head, not truly understanding her friend. Claire was simply too fucked to be of much use for the next several hours. She either needed to calm down for a while or just role with it and accept the fact that her day was going to be all about sex, or at least more about sex than it usually was.

However, for Sonja, her purpose was clear. She borrowed clothes from Claire, no longer having an outfit that would fit her expanded curves. Not that Claire minded. She was happy to share.

Not that Sonja needed much. She found a tiny pair of leather shorts, the kind that did not cover her entire ass and that looked more like underwear than actual daywear. She also found a pair of high-heeled boots, also in leather, that meant all the way up to just below her knees. They hugged her calves perfectly and gave her skin a little extra protection.

The last step was for Sonja to pull on her leather jacket she had arrived in. She giggled as she zipped it up over her tits, although she left the zipper incredibly low, showing off a good portion of her expanded tits and the deep valley of her cleavage. She did not bother with a bra or other top. As far as she was concerned, she did not need to wear anything else.

Andrew was at his computer when Sonja said her goodbye. She gave him a long kiss with plenty of tongue, but otherwise said nothing. Then she walked out of the house, grabbing her motorcycle helmet along the way. Claire watched her friend leave from the window, still topless and giving anyone who walked by a show. That was assuming they could keep their eyes off the blonde beauty climbing onto her motorcycle.

"Fuck that's nice," Sonja moaned as the bike rumbled to life beneath her, the vibrations sending another spike of arousal through her. She was definitely going to be looking for a man to fuck soon. But first she needed to start looking for the future vessel of the Goddess. As a bimbo, Sonja had little idea of what she was doing. But she was certain she would know what to do when the time came. Being such a hot and slutty woman, things tended to just work out that way.

When Sonja first pulled up to the house, she had been a woman without a purpose. Now, Sonja was a happy bimbo on a mission. She might not have understood much of anything anymore, but she was certain to enjoy herself as she searched high and low for the perfect woman to bring the Goddess into this world. She and Claire were but messengers, spreading peace, happiness, and bimbodom to all who would accept the message. This was the way. This was the purpose of the Icon of the Eqo.

But Sonja's bimbo journey was just beginning. Her transformation was complete, but her path would take her wherever she was needed until the Goddess of the bimbos had returned to this world. Sonja would have it no other way. Then again, as a bimbo, she did not know of another way. This was who she was and as she rode away, there was a happy smile on her face.

3

BIMBO QUEEN

"Yes," Sonja moaned as the man thrust his cock into her pussy from behind.

She did not know the man's name, but she did not care about that. All that mattered was that he had a big cock and that he knew how to use it. And with her bent over her motorcycle, her leather jacket open to reveal her big tits, her leather shorts down around one of her ankles, Sonja could not have been happier.

Ever since leaving Claire and Andrew's house, she had traveled, searching for the perfect vessel for the Eqo Goddess to be reborn into. And each stop of her traveling resulted in moments like this one, where she got fucked long and hard. It was what she lived for, beyond her need to find the right woman.

Normally Sonja would be moaning with calls for her man of the moment to fuck her harder and faster. He could even throw in a few slaps on her ass. She would love all of it. Sex was the one thing Sonja could still call herself an expert in, partly because she was obsessed with it, but also because she had so much of it. It was a slow day when she could count the number of times she had been fucked in a day on one hand. Then again, she struggled to count beyond 10, because she forgot she could use her toes too.

However, this was not the time or the place. She had parked her motorcycle in an alley. She had nothing against being fucked in public, but getting arrested would prevent her from performing her sacred task. Besides, she had a good vantage point of the street, even if she and her exposed tits were hidden in the shadow of the alley. And it was the street where she was looking, her eyes scanning the passersby, keeping a lookout for the one.

Sonja had no idea what qualities she was looking for. The perfect vessel was hard to define. There had been some women who had been close. Sonja knew that much at least. But they were not perfect. There was always something missing, some quality that the woman lacked. They all would have made fine bimbos, but Sonja was looking for the woman who would become the Bimbo Queen.

It was difficult to keep her attention on the street. Sonja wanted nothing more than to give herself over to the man who was fucking her. He had a nice cock and she figured he deserved more. However, there was no way she could give him her full attention right now. Somehow Sonja knew she was close. She felt it like a sixth sense. Her travels had been fun, especially the way she often traded sex for a bed or a few gallons of gas. It was amazing what a man was willing to give her after she gave him a ride.

"Here it comes you stupid slut," the man groaned with pleasure as his cock surged with cum.

Normally Sonja would have closed her eyes and let her own orgasm take her, relishing the erotic energy flowing through her body. But she kept her eyes open, looking out at the street, although she could not help but let out a moan as her body shook in response to the pleasure coursing through her body. The endorphin rush she got from cumming was better than anything else she could imagine, but that did not stop her from fulfilling her mission.

And it was a good thing she kept her eyes open, because otherwise she would have missed the woman she had been searching for. Sonja only saw her for a moment, watching a small woman walk by, her frizzy hair and glasses barely hiding the extreme acne on her face. Her clothes were as unbimbo-like as they came, her white button-up blouse and khaki pants fitting her horrendously, making her look more man than woman. It was only her size and feminine face that made it clear she was a woman.

In all her short-lived bimbo experience, Sonja never would have guessed that the perfect vessel would look like that. She had expected the woman to be somewhere on the bimbo spectrum already. It made sense in a way. Although Sonja was never someone who trusted her own sense now that she was a bimbo. She was much too dumb for that. But where she lacked in intelligence, she excelled at looking hot as fuck and being able to get a man hard with a single sultry look.

"That was fun," Sonja said as she slid her leather shorts back up her legs. The man who had just cum in her was still a little out of it, his cock still dominating his thought processes. Sonja knew what that was like from the opposite side. She had spent plenty of time as a cock-dumb slut, her already bimbofied brain refusing to work after a hard fucking.

"Fuck, you're gonna make me hard again," the man said, his voice so deep Sonja could almost feel the rumble in her chest.

"I have that effect on people." Sonja smiled as she zipped up her jacket. Not that she sipped it up all the way. She only brought the zipper up high enough to make sure her nipples were covered. Her girls liked to breathe, which was why she unzipped the jacket to begin with. And her man of the moment had enjoyed playing with them before he finally bent her over the bike so he could fuck her properly. "But I gotta go meet someone."

Had Sonja asked for money, the man would have assumed she was a prostitute. She had that kind of look about her. And he would have assumed the person she needed to meet was her pimp. He had no idea that Sonja was on a quasi-religious mission, finding the woman who would someday host the Goddess in her body, becoming the queen of the bimbos.

Without another word, Sonja straddled her motorcycle and fired it up. The engine roared to life and the vibrations she felt through the saddle were almost enough to make her cum again. There had been multiple near misses along her journey from her closing her eyes for a moment to enjoy a small orgasm. Thankfully no one was hurt. But even though Sonja was ready to cum again, she knew better than to indulge herself now.

Sonja rode out of the alley just fast enough to maintain her balance on the bike. She was not far behind the woman she had been searching for, but she did not need to race after her either. Somehow Sonja understood that she needed to be careful. While this woman was the perfect vessel, she would need persuading to return with Sonja.

As Sonja approached, she got a better look at the woman she had been searching for. The woman was small, but it was more that she was rail thin. Her clothing draped off of her, swallowing her up and making her look even smaller. She also hunched over, making her appear shorter than she really was. And as Sonja rode up alongside the woman, it was clear as day that she was just about the nerdiest woman Sonja had ever seen, and that was including the time in her past life she spent as a librarian.

"Hi," Sonja said, trying to get the woman's attention. She had left her helmet on the back of her bike, her blonde hair flowing behind her as she tried to match the woman's walking speed.

However, the woman kept her head down and kept walking.

Sonja was not sure if the woman heard her or if she just assumed Sonja was talking to someone else.

Knowing she needed to get the woman's attention, Sonja drove up the block, leaving the woman behind her. She needed time to park and then confront the woman head on. That was the only way she was going to get through the woman's shell.

Off her bike, Sonja stepped onto the sidewalk and positioned herself directly in front of the woman as she approached. She stood there, her feet shoulder width apart and her hands on her hips, waiting. Sonja got lots of looks from the other people on the sidewalk, but they simply walked by her, turning their heads to either check out her tits or her ass. Both were spectacular and worth looking at, but Sonja paid them no attention. She was on a mission.

The woman kept walking with her head down, not seeing Sonja stand there. That was until she stopped just short of running into the bimbo, her eyes getting a close up view of Sonja's exposed cleavage.

"Hi," Sonja said again.

This time it was clear the woman heard her. She looked up into Sonja's face and stared blankly, not understanding what was happening.

"Um, hi," the woman said meekly. She was not sure how to respond. It was only then that she realized that the "hi" she heard earlier came from this woman and that she was talking to her. "You were trying to get my attention. Did I drop something?"

The woman looked behind her, expecting to see something on the sidewalk. However, the sidewalk was abnormally clean, without a hint of anything, not even any litter that someone had thoughtlessly thrown aside.

"I've been looking for you," Sonja said. "You should come with me."

The woman sputtered at Sonja's bold suggestion. She did not

even know who this woman was or what she wanted. Although, as the woman looked at Sonja, she had to admit she was a beautiful woman. There was something inside of the woman that awakened to Sonja's presence. There was an understanding that blossomed inside of her that Sonja held the keys to her success and happiness. Not that the woman could explain any of that. It was just a gut feeling.

"Who are you?" the woman asked. Even if she somehow knew that she would be joining this woman wherever she went, there was still a need for information.

Sonja giggled before she answered, "I'm Sonja. And I'm here to make all your dreams come true."

The woman's face turned red at the thought. All of her dreams? That was impossible. But the woman could still hope.

"Um, hi, Sonja," the woman said. She held out her hand, expecting to shake Sonja's hand. "My name is Sandy Peters."

However, Sonja was not interested in shaking hands. Instead, she pulled Sandy into a hug, wrapping her arms around the thin woman and pressing her into her large tits. Sonja would have kissed her too, but she had a feeling that Sandy was not ready for that yet. They still needed to develop a rapport, but Sonja was going to do everything she could to make Sandy comfortable with the future that awaited her.

Sandy stood there, pressed against Sonja's big tits, wondering what was happening to her. None of this seemed real. She had never been an outgoing person. It was one reason why she chose a career in technical writing. It allowed her to follow some of her passions, learning about new technology as she wrote about it, translating technical specifics into language understood by laymen. But it also left her cutoff from her peers and left her dreaming for a better life.

It was no secret what Sandy really wanted in life. At least it was not a secret she kept from herself. Instead, she went to sleep every night dreaming about what her life would be like if she had been different, if she had been an extrovert, if she had been pretty, if she had a body like Sonja's. There was the constant question of what if running through her mind.

"Will you come with me to make your dreams come true?" Sonja asked. She had yet to release Sandy from her embrace.

Sandy did not know what to say. Her rational mind was screaming at her to say no, to deny that any of this was possible. It should not have been possible. There was no way that Sonja could actually produce what she had offered. And yet, Sandy could not stop herself from nodding her head, giving permission for Sonja to lead her away from her life of technical drudgery and toward something brighter and happier.

"Oh goodie," Sonja said, adding a giggle in for good measure.

Sandy had never ridden on a motorcycle before. It had always seemed too dangerous. But somehow she felt safe with Sonja. She did not complain as Sonja helped her onto the back of her bike. Sandy was given the helmet to wear. Sonja would make do without, at least for now. The bimbo was sure to find the means to obtain another helmet soon enough. She had her femininity and thirst for sex to fall back on.

Before Sandy knew it, she had her arms around Sonja's torso, holding on for dear life as Sonja drove away. The motorcycle was not strictly made for two people to ride, but they both managed to fit on. Then again, if Sandy ever ended up looking like Sonja in any way, she might not fit. Between a bigger ass and much bigger tits, it might be difficult for them both to fit on the motorcycle.

It was only later, once Sonja had pulled over at a roadside motel for the night that Sandy started to question what she was doing. She had been walking home from work when Sonja found her. She had not even bothered to return to her apartment. She had just gotten on the bike with her guide, leaving her old life behind. The odd part was that Sandy felt no love lost about any of that. She had no desire to return to her old life.

That gut feeling was guiding her and it said to follow Sonja. She could not explain it, but she did not want to explain it either. It felt too good to even consider trying to return to her old life. This was the adventure she had always dreamed of.

Sandy leaned against the motorcycle as Sonja checked them in. She could not understand what was taking so long. The motel was not busy. Paying for a room should not have taken more than a few minutes. Little did Sandy understand that Sonja was paying for their room with her body, sucking off the manager with a promise of more if he could get it up again.

"Finally," Sandy said, slightly annoyed by the long wait when Sonja reappeared. Sonja smiled, licking her lips, knowing that it would only be a few days before her charge would be performing similar acts.

If Sonja were not such a bimbo, she would have regretted not bringing the Icon with her. That small sculpture would have easily fit in her saddle bags. Sandy could already be well on her way to fulfilling her true purpose in life. Instead, however, they were forced to travel back the way Sonja had come, returning to Claire and Andrew so that Sandy could touch the Icon of the Eqo and fill herself with the Goddess, becoming a queen of bimbos.

"Don't worry, I've got plenty of energy left for you," Sonja said as she dangled the key, for it was still a key and not a keycard. "This way."

Sandy followed her guide to their room. When Sonja opened the door, they were greeted by a relatively clean room with one large king-sized bed. Sandy immediately stood up straight, recognizing the problem with their room for the night. There was only one bed. Sandy was up for an adventure, but she was now second guessing herself. She did not know Sonja very well and now that she thought about it, she probably should have gone home first to pack a few things. There was not room for much, but she could have packed a change of clothes into a backpack.

"Where's my bed?" Sandy asked as Sonja climbed onto the bed and posed herself for Sandy's benefit.

Sonja did not say anything. Instead, she raised a finger and motioned Sandy forward, wanting Sandy to join her on the bed.

A fire erupted inside Sandy. She had never considered sex with a woman before. She had always thought herself straight, only thinking about sexy women out of jealousy, wishing she could look that good. But Sandy was already starting to discover that there was more to her life now than she had ever been able to imagine.

Sandy stepped forward without even thinking about it. She took another step and then another. And before she knew it, she was standing beside Sonja, her eyes fixated on the bimbo's tits. They were big and round and they were now out in the open. Sonja had lowered her zipper to free her girls, her hard nipples sliding into view. Sandy's eyes became fixated on Sonja's cleavage, unable to look away.

"I want to show you what the future holds for you," Sonja said as she beckoned Sandy to join her on the bed.

Moving almost as if she was in a trance, Sandy climbed onto the bed to join her bimbo guide. The moment that Sonja's plump lips touched her own, she was lost to the pleasure. Sandy had never figured a woman could make her feel so good. And it was just a kiss. But that was just the beginning for the two women. Sonja was an expert when it came to sex, no matter who her partner was. Her recent experience in addition to the sexual knowledge the Icon had imbued her with meant she could make anyone squeal with sexual delight.

And that was exactly what Sandy did. Sonja took her time, but Sandy squealed over and over and she came again and again. It took a few hours, but by the time Sandy drifted off to sleep, she was naked, her pale skin flushed with arousal, and had cum more times than she could count.

Sonja managed to get out of bed without disturbing the snoozing Sandy, throwing on her jacket and shorts, before she returned to the manager's office to make sure their room remained paid for the night. Besides, Sonja had not cum since she had been railed from behind by the man in the alley. She needed an orgasm of her own. Sandy was not yet schooled in the ways of the bimbo and could not yet give as well as she received.

It took several days for Sonja and Sandy to make their way to Claire and Andrew's house. Each day was filled with long hours on the motorcycle, taking breaks to eat and to engage in a little fingering action. Sonja could get Sandy off with ease, but she was also teaching the nerd how to reciprocate. Sandy's fingers were not nearly as nimble when it came to sex, but she was learning quickly.

The one area where Sonja maintained the heavy lifting was when it came to paying for their motel rooms and even their meals. Sandy never had to lift a finger when it came to that sort of thing. A few men had eyed Sandy for a possible three-some, but Sonja always found a way to avoid it. Somehow she knew that Sandy was not ready for that yet. She was not a slut and she definitely was not a bimbo. At least she was none of those things yet. Once the Icon changed her, that might change, but even Sonja had no idea what her Goddess personi-fied would be like. She only knew that she had a mission to complete.

When Sonja finally stopped the motorcycle in front of Claire and Andrew's house, she let out a sigh, knowing that her mission was almost complete. By now, Sandy was well versed in getting onto and off the bike and she slid off with practiced ease, instinctually knowing that this was their final destination. She did not know how she knew. Sonja had never specifically told her where they were going. But she knew this was where she needed to go.

And it became even more obvious when a slutty looking bimbo raced out of the house and wrapped Sonja up in a big embrace, filled with mashing big tits together, hugging, and kissing. Sandy was left standing awkwardly, not sure what she should do. Clearly Sonja and this other bimbo knew each other well. But Sandy had also started to figure she knew Sonja pretty well. After all, the pair had been traveling together and when they were not sleeping or riding, they were usually having sex.

Not that Sandy was complaining. She might have felt awkward, especially being around another insanely well-endowed bimbo, but that seemed to leave some amount of promise for her. It gave her hope that her days as a flat-chested waif were at an end. Although she had no concept of the cost of plastic surgery to get her up to Sonja's level. The bimbo had not exactly been forthcoming about what her future entailed. Then again, they had been too busy having sex all the time to really talk about it and the noise while riding prevented most conversation.

"Claire, this is Sandy," Sonja said once the bimbo make-out session had finished. "She's the vessel I was sent to find."

Vessel. Sandy had heard Sonja say that before, although never right in front of her before. She had heard her mumble that word in her sleep, but she never understood what Sonja meant by it. Sandy had never considered herself a vessel before. But the way she had felt these last couple days did leave her sensing that there was something expected of her in all of this. She could not even begin to understand what this new life meant for her, but she knew that her life would soon be more enjoyable than she could have ever imagined.

"You're so cute," Claire squealed as she wrapped Sandy into a similar embrace. However, it was obvious that calling Sandy cute was being nice. The only part of her that could be considered cute was her diminutive size and that was mostly an illusion.

"Thanks," Sandy answered as she lightly returned Claire's hug, clapping the bimbo's back awkwardly. "So what's going to happen here?"

"Your future is going to happen," Sonja answered.

Sandy did not know what to say to that, but she was now used to Sonja's way of speaking. Half the time the bimbo sounded somewhat normal, although with an ethereal echo in her voice, almost as if her words were being forced out of her. The rest of the time Sonja sounded like a complete bimbo, which was what Sandy figured her new friend really was.

Sandy said nothing as she let herself be guided into the house. She vaguely heard Claire speak as they entered, "Andrew is out right now. Should we wait for him?"

"Our Goddess has waited long enough," Sonja answered.

Sandy found herself being sat down on a couch in a nondescript living room. There were two other chairs. Sonja sat in one of the chairs, but Claire flitted off into another room to retrieve something. Or at least that was what Sandy had gathered. She felt oddly disjointed, almost like she was merely a bystander in all of this. She was a bystander in her own body, watching what unfolded in front of her, but not fully being present in the moment. It was a strange sensation, but it was also pleasant, making Sandy happy that she had thrown her life into complete chaos for this adventure.

Claire returned a minute later with the Icon in her hands. She placed the stone sculpture on the coffee table in front of Sandy and then took her seat in the second chair.

Sandy found her gaze directed at the Icon. She had little understanding of what it was. All she could tell was it looked ancient. She felt mesmerized by it, much in the way she had previously been mesmerized by Sonja's cleavage. Only this time, it was much stronger. Sandy could not look away. Not that she wanted to. Instead, she found her gaze getting drawn in deeper and deeper.

"What am I supposed to do?" Sandy asked. But already her body was betraying her. Her hand reached out toward it, her body leaning forward, preparing to make contact. Even if Sandy did not know it herself, her body knew what her future held and how to get it.

"Touch it and become the woman you were meant to be," Sonja answered, her voice echoing through the room, drumming on Sandy's brain.

The moment Sandy's fingers made contact with the cold stone of the sculpture, her eyes rolled up into the back of her head. She continued to sit there, maintaining contact as her eyelids fluttered. It was as if Sandy's hand and arm were acting as a conduit for the power of the Icon to flow into her.

That was mostly true, although the reality was slightly different. Sandy's soul was the exact opposite of the Goddess that lived within the Icon. With Claire and Sonja, their souls had needed only partial modifications, replacing only parts and not the whole. But with Sandy, her soul was replaced entirely. The essence of the Goddess flowed into her and pushed out what had been Sandy. The conduit between Sandy and the Icon moved both ways, sending Sandy's soul to reside within the sculpture and giving the Goddess free rein in her body.

"Whoa," Sandy finally said when she pulled her hand back. Her fingers went to her head, trying to understand what had happened to her. She felt different. She felt sexier, at least on the inside. But she still felt like herself. Her soul had been replaced, but Sandy was still her, at least in mind and body. It was just now she held the soul of a bimbo Goddess within her. And it was now that she understood why she had been referred to as a vessel. She understood her future, even if she had no idea what it would look like.

However, unlike the transformations of both Claire and

Sonja, Sandy immediately found herself growing tired. She did not even have a chance to say anything more before she dropped to the side, laying out on the couch, her eyes closed, sleep taking her.

Claire and Sonja were confused, although they had no idea what to expect when all of this began. All they knew was that their roles had been completed. Sonja had found the vessel and the Goddess had been unleashed. In the end, they carried Sandy into the spare bedroom, striping her down and letting her sleep in the nude. Andrew had it made up to be Sonja's room originally, having moved or sold off most of Sonja's previous belongings. For tonight, Sonja planned to spend her time in Claire's bed, with Andrew. It was where she was meant to be, at least for now.

When Andrew returned, he checked in on Sandy, having figured out most of what had happened from observation and the piecemeal bimbo-speak he had picked up from both Claire and Sonja babbling about it all. Had he realized that Sonja would be returning, he would have made sure he was home for the big return. He was actually shocked that Sonja had found the woman she was looking for. It seemed like her mission could have taken years instead of only a couple weeks.

Not that Andrew was complaining about having two bimbos at his beck and call now. He very much enjoyed the bimbofied Claire, but he had to admit that two bimbos was definitely better than one. And he made sure to fuck both of them hard and long, enjoying putting his increased stamina to work. That increase had been needed with the amount of sex Claire demanded of him.

As Sandy slept in the room next door, her body went through a massive shift. It started at a structural level, her bones growing and transforming, giving her the base from which a true bimbo could be made. Sandy was made taller, her limbs gaining better proportionality with the rest of her body. Her pelvis widened, giving her a better platform in which to build an hourglass figure with.

But it was not all growth. The magic working its way through Sandy's body also decided there were some unneeded items. Specifically, two ribs on each side simply dissolved away, disappearing to allow for an even smaller waist and an even more exaggerated figure. It had been good that she had been stripped bare, because her widened hips never would have fit in her old khaki pants.

Once Sandy's skeleton had been fixed, her musculature began to shift and change. Her muscles were what allowed her to be the perfect bimbo specimen that she was turning into and that meant she needed to be able to move and fuck to the best of her ability. Her ass filled out with improved muscle tone. Her back muscles strengthened to better hold up her future tits. Her core strengthened to help make up for the fact she was now missing four ribs. And she all around gained strength and stamina to make sure she was as fuckable as possible.

Next came a redistribution of fat. Not that Sandy had much, being as thin as she was, but she had a little tiny extra bit around her belly that was moved into her chest and her butt. It was small, but noticeable. It also helped to further highlight her waspish waist and even give her some muscle definition in her abs.

With all of those things taken care of, the magic moved to the more cosmetic changes. First on the list was giving Sandy tits. She had never had the need to wear a bra. On the day she had been picked up by Sonja, she had not been wearing one, although she did most of the time to better fit in. It was only when she wore heavier fabrics that she went without.

Sandy's tits ballooned off her chest, turning into large balls that looked almost bolted on. They were real, but looked as if they were fake. And there was no need for a bra. Her new girls could stand up all on their own, the magic that created them making sure they would never sag or cause back pain.

Next came Sandy's ass. It finished filling out, giving her a bubble butt that matched her widened hips. People would turn their heads when she passed, either to see her from the front, to see her impressive tits that were even bigger than Claire and Sonja's sets, or to see her ass, which would bounce and sway with every step she took for the rest of her life.

Of course, that sway would be exaggerated by Sandy's need for certain kinds of footwear from now on. Her feet and lower legs were remodeled to make the wearing of high heels not only preferred, but almost necessary. Sandy would be able to walk without heels, but she would always do so by walking on her toes. The only time her heels would ever support her weight from now on was if she wore high heels, the higher the better.

As her skin began to gain a darkened glow, her hair was dramatically altered. The frizzy brown that had defined her life was replaced with long flowing locks of blonde hair. Most of her hair was colored platinum blonde, but there were a few darker highlights mixed in to provide a more textured appearance. But it was not just length, color, and composition that changed. She gained even more volume, giving her a mass of hair that would take a normal person hours to care for properly. Not that the new Sandy would mind that. Her appearance was now going to be one of her most important attributes.

The final physical changes happened to Sandy's face. The acne that had plagued her all her life disappeared. Her skin became smooth and unblemished. The scars that had pockmarked her skin faded away entirely. But along with her skin improving, her whole facial structure changed. Her nose became smaller and more petite, turning up slightly at the end. Her cheekbones grew more prominent, giving her a heart shaped face that was almost impossible to look away from, assuming someone could stop staring at her tits or ass.

Sandy's eyes grew bigger and her lashes lengthened, giving her an almost doll-like appearance. And even though her eyes were closed, her blue-gray eyes lost all hint of gray, becoming more brilliant, making sure that if someone was able to take in all of her body, they would find her eyes almost entrancing.

The final physical change came to Sandy's lips. They grew out, plumping up and making it clear what they were best suited for. Where before Sandy sported thin lips that no one took a second look at, now she had lips that almost dominated her face. They would have if her eyes and other facial features had not transformed as well. Her lips had become plump pleasure pillows that looked like they belonged wrapped around a cock.

However, the physical transformation was only one part of a larger process. Up until this point, Sandy had only changed physically. Had she woken up then, she might have had a body she could only dream about, but she still would have been the nerdy technical writer on the inside. She would have had no idea how to actually use her body and she would have shied away from the attention it would have given her. All that needed to change.

But that was where the Goddess came in. Her soul entered Sandy's mind and made wholesale changes. All those facts and figures that had made her a great technical writer were erased, completely wiped away to make room for more important matters. Every part of Sandy's brain was touched by the Goddess that had taken up residence within her. Her introverted nature was replaced with an outgoing bubbliness that would make Sandy the center of attention wherever she went.

Every nerdy aspect of Sandy was replaced, making her image-obsessed and vivacious. And that was before the entirely to human knowledge about sex and sexual pleasure was uploaded into her brain. If Sandy had remained the intelligent woman she had been before, she would have been able to write the definitive book on sex. Instead, she would only be able to live that experience. Not that living that way could be considered a bad thing. She and everyone around her would certainly enjoy it.

Just as the last change to her mind was made, her eyes fluttered open. Morning had arrived and with it a new person.

Queen Sandi opened her eyes and smiled. She sat up and looked over her body, enjoying every new curve. She ran her long-nailed fingers down her flank, enjoying the way her body responded to her touch. She had not even seen her reflection in a mirror yet, but just looking down at her body was enough to make her wet.

When Sandi stood up, perched up on her toes, she licked her lips, knowing that she had a body built for one thing. She was sex personified. No man or woman could deny her if she put her mind to it. Her powers of seduction were infinite and unstoppable. And she thanked her lucky stars to have a new vessel to live in. And she would live for a long time, powered by her magic, maintaining her youthful appearance for years and years as she built up a whole army of bimbos, not to fight, but to fuck, all the way across the globe.

The lack of clothing covering her body did not bother her as Sandi walked out of the bedroom. She was perfectly content to be completely naked. Clothes were meant to enhance her sex appeal and not actually cover her body. She knew that deep down in her core. It was one of the rules she now lived by.

Walking into the other bedroom in the house, she found Claire and Sonja sleeping on either side of Andrew. He looked exhausted as he snored deeply. However, the two bimbos on the bed woke up, almost as if they could sense their new queen's presence. They each sat up and then turned so that they were on their knees before Sandi.

Sandi smiled and silently beckoned them to rise. She reached out her arms and they hurried toward her, happy to press their nubile bodies up against her own. They pressed their big tits into her even larger tits and hugged her back. They looked up into her eyes, entranced by her bimbo beauty, rising far and above their own. In each and every way, Sandi was hotter and more bimbo-esque than they could ever hope to be. But that was as it was supposed to be. Sandi was their bimbo queen and she deserved to be hotter than them.

"Thank you for finding me and freeing me," Sandi said, her voice coming out high pitched and breathy. It sounded like she was seducing her charges, which she was without even trying. Both bimbos at her side were as wet as could be, ready for anything. They were always ready, but now they were even more so.

"You're welcome, Your Majesty," Claire and Sonja said in unison as they continued to look upon Sandi with reverence.

"And now I must fuck this man," Sandi said as she pulled her arms away from her bimbos and stepped forward toward the bed.

"His name is Andrew," Claire offered, not knowing what the queen remembered of Sandy's life before. She was certain that Andrew had been mentioned during the brief meeting before, but as a bimbo, she knew her memory was likely faulty. She was too dumb and too pretty to worry about it though.

"Andrew," Sandi whispered. "He will do nicely."

Andrew started to wake as Sandi climbed onto the bed. She let her fingernails lightly slide up the soles of Andrew's feet, making him shiver. He opened his eyes and was faced with the most beautiful woman he had ever seen before. Claire as a bimbo was great, but this woman was even better. Where Claire was a 10, Sandi was an 11. There was no beating her.

"I believe I want you to be the first man I fuck," Sandi cooed as she crawled forward, letting her big tits hang beneath her. Not that they did much hanging, but they looked amazing nonetheless. Of course, the odd part of all of this was the fact that Sandi was technically a virgin. She had sex with Sonja on the way here, but she had never been with a man before, even before she had been turned into a bimbo queen.

However, none of that mattered anymore once she straddled Andrew, his cock hard as a rock as it stood straight up as he laid there on the bed. He looked up at Sandi, his eyes struggling to look away from her amazing tits, but when they managed to flit away for a moment, he was transfixed by her large blue eyes and cocksucking lips. Even if he had wanted to say no, there was no way that word could leave his lips. Luckily, he very much wanted to have the personification of bimbo perfection ride his morning wood.

"Oh, that is heavenly," Sandi cooed as she sank down onto his length, his shaft splitting her open for the first time. And for a moment, that was enough, just to feel him filling her. But then the magic of the Goddess went to work, increasing his size, his girth, filling her almost to the point of being too big.

Andrew cried out as his body filled with pleasure. He had no idea what was happening to his cock, but he loved it. He had no sense that he was being given a permanent upgrade.

But once he was of size, Sandi got to work, bucking and grinding against her mount, riding him like a saddle. His hands came up and took hold of her tits. They easily dwarfed his hands, but she loved how he touched her nonetheless.

With both of her hands, she reached back and beckoned her bimbo charges to join her. They snapped to attention and jumped onto the bed. Soon Claire and Sonja were pressed up against her, kissing her, licking her, worshiping her. For that was their purpose now. The Goddess had been released and now she lived within Sandi. And as bimbos, it was their job to serve and worship their queen.

It did not take long for the four participants to collapse into a pile of limbs as they all found ways to pleasure each other. But all the while, Sandi fucked Andrew, keeping his now oversized cock inside of her.

And the moment she finally came, having tested the stamina of everyone else, all four of them came together, triggered by the magic that continued to course through the room. Queen Sandi's cries of passion were echoed by the others as they were all gripped together in the throes of orgasm, pleasure cascading through their bodies, flowing from one to another as they each came harder than they ever had before.

And when it was finally over, once Sandi had her initial fill, she dismounted and pulled herself free from the mass of limbs, happy with her new life.

"Bring me a dress to wear, something appropriately slutty for a queen," Sandi commanded.

Claire jumped up and immediately went to her closet to find something appropriate for her bimbo queen to wear. When Claire returned, she held a tight yellow minidress with a deep scoop neckline and a hem that would barely fall past the curve of Sandi's bimbo ass.

"Perfect," Sandi said, patting Claire on the head.

Sonja appeared a moment later holding a pair of yellow heels that matched the dress. They fit Sandi perfectly, allowing her to stand properly for the first time since she had awoken with her new body.

"Get dressed, girls," Sandi announced. "The man can stay here and recuperate, but we must go out and recruit more bimbos. And we need to find men to fill out my kingdom. It's time to bring back the Eqo way of life."

"Yes, your majesty," The two bimbos and Andrew said in unison. They were all in awe of Queen Sandi.

It was impossible to know exactly what would come next. Would the bimbo queen manage to carve out a kingdom for herself, creating a world where all the women were bimbos and all the men well-hung? Could such a society actually last? It was all unknown. But even Sandy would have been happy with this turn of events. She would gladly take a back seat so that she could be Sandi, queen of the bimbos. For her and her bimbo charges, life was better this way. And now they just needed to show the world the truth they had learned. Bimbo was better.

ABOUT THE AUTHOR

Sadie Thatcher is a longtime author of erotic fiction, especially related to transformations and bimbofication. She likes to say "I have thrown off the shackles of my conservative upbringing and now write erotic stories."

She maintains a special blog devoted to her writings, including a behind the scenes look at her writing process, and bimbos in general, as well as highlights works by other authors. They can be found at:

https://authorsadiethatcher.tumblr.com

 twitter.com/Sadie_Thatcher

Bimbo Dome

Acting the Part

Subliminal Society

Inheritance

Company Morale

His Bimbo Girlfriend

The Bimbo Room

The Bimbos of Blossom

Dr. Jekyll and Missy Hyde

Second Chance

From M&As To T&A

Trading Places

The Bimbo Nutcracker Suite

Milked and Herded

Fitting In

Clowning Around

Transformative Ink

Choices

Rival Competition

Alien Womanhood

Invasion

The Princess and the Bimbo

Bimbo Labyrinth

The Legend of the Werebimbo

Power and Corruption

The Simulation

The Curse of Playing Bimbo Tag

The Curse of Playing Bimbo Tag: Jenna or Jenni

The Bimbo Professor: The Curse of Playing Bimbo Tag Book 3

Anything for the Job

Anything for the Job 2

Anything for His Job

The Bimbo in the Mirror

The Bimbo in the Mirror 2

Astrid and the Bimbo Bee

Bella and the Bimbo Bee

Cali and the Bimbo Bee

Desiree and the Bimbo Bee

Ember and the Bimbo Bee

Fiona and the Bimbo Bee

The Intern

The Lawyer

The Hacker

Cause & Effect

Witless Protection

Stealing Sally

Trial and Error

Beta Testing

Exposed

Bimbo for a Weekend

Bimbo for a Week

Bimbo for Life

Fake It Until You Make It Season 1

Simple and Fun Volume 1

Simple and Fun Volume 2

Simple and Fun Volume 3

Simple and Fun Volume 4

Simple and Fun Volume 5

Simple and Fun Volume 6

Bimbo Halloween

Bimbo Christmas

Bimbo Technology

Dorm Room Bimbo

Carissa's Magic Pen

Spirit Walk

Muscle Memory

The Case of the Bimbo Wife

Changes

Changes 2

New Year New You

The Bimbo Dream

The Wedding Gift

The Cure

Backfire

Bim & Bo Yoga

Wishing for Each Other

Bimbo Roots

A Bimbo at Oktoberfest

The Lost Bet

The Fountain

Bimbo Ghost

Sugar and Spice and Everything Nice

Basic Bimbo

A Helping Hand

The Bimbo Experience

The Bimbo Experience 2

The Bimbo Experience 3some

The 4th Bimbo Experience

Bimbo Genes

Bimbo Genes II: The Virus

The Bimbo Genes III: The Epidemic

Bimbo Juice: Blue Raspberry

Bimbo Juice: Grape

Bimbo Juice: Mango

Bimbo Juice: Pineapple

Bimbo Juice: Red Apple

Bimbo Juice: Veggie

Bimbo Juice Gone Wild: The Muse

Bimbo Juice Gone Wild: Street Racer

Bimbo Juice Gone Wild: Score

Bimbos of the Traveling Earrings: Book 1

Bimbos of the Traveling Earrings: Book 2

Bimbos of the Traveling Earrings: Book 3

Bimbos of the Traveling Earrings: Book 4

Bimbo Party: Kennedy

Bimbo Party: Esme

Bimbo Party: Ariana

Bimbo Party: Tara

Workout Buddies

Wishful Thinking

Wanting More

Bimbo Harem: Annabelle

The Message

Bimbo Queen

Bachelorette

www.ingramcontent.com/pod-product-compliance
Lightning Source LLC
Chambersburg PA
CBHW060453160726
47992CB00003B/1201